More books about
My Naughty Little Sister

My Naughty Little Sister

My Naughty Little Sister and Bad Harry

When My Naughty Little Sister Was Good

My Naughty Little Sister's Friends

More Naughty Little Sister Stories

DOROTHY EDWARDS

ILLUSTRATED BY

Shirley Hughes

EGMONT

For Jane and the two Franks

EGMONT
We bring stories to life

First published in Great Britain 1970
by Methuen Children's Books Ltd
This edition published 2017
by Egmont UK Limited
The Yellow Building, 1 Nicholas Road
London, W11 4AN

ISBN 978 1 4052 5338 3

www.egmont.co.uk

A CIP catalogue record for this title is available from the British Library

Printed and bound in Great Britain by the CPI Group

24933/24

Contents

1   The very first story   1

2   My Naughty Little Sister and the
    book-little-boy   10

3   My Naughty Little Sister and
    poor Charlie Cocoa   19

4   My Naughty Little Sister and the
    big girl's bed   34

5   The cross photograph   46

6   My Naughty Little Sister wins
    a prize   57

7   My Naughty Little Sister and
    the baby   79

8   Bad Harry's haircut   88

9   My Naughty Little Sister shows off   99

10 My Naughty Little Sister and the
    solid silver watch   111

11 Mrs Cocoa's white visitor   122

1. The very first story

A very long time ago, when I was a little girl, I didn't have a naughty little sister at all. I was a child all on my own. I had a father and a mother of course, but I hadn't any other little brothers or sisters – I was quite alone.

I was a very lucky little girl because I had a dear grannie and a dear grandad and lots of kind aunts and uncles to make a fuss of me. They played games with me, and gave me toys and took me for walks, and bought me ice-creams and told me stories, but I hadn't got a little sister.

Well now, one day, when I was a child on my own, I went to stay with my kind godmother-aunt in the country. My kind godmother-aunt was very good to me. She took me out every day to see the farm animals and to pick flowers, and she read stories to me, and let me cook little cakes and jam tarts in her oven, and I was very, very happy. I didn't want to go home one bit.

Then, one day, my godmother-aunt said, 'Here is a letter from your father, and what do you think he says?'

My aunt was smiling and smiling.

'What do you think he says?' she asked. 'He says that you have a little baby sister waiting for you at home!'

I *was* excited! I said, 'I think I had better go home at once, don't you?' and my kind godmother-aunt said, 'I think you had indeed.' And she took me home that very day!

My aunt took me on a train and a bus and another bus, and then I was home!

And, do you know, before I'd even got indoors, I heard a waily-waily noise coming from the house, and my godmother-aunt said, 'That is your new sister.'

'Waah-waah,' my little sister was saying, 'waah-waah.'

I was surprised to think that such a very new child could make so much noise, and I ran straight indoors and straight upstairs and straight into my mother's bedroom. And there was my good kind mother sitting up in bed smiling and smiling, and there, in a

cot that used to be my old cot, was my new cross little sister crying and crying!

My mother said, 'Sh-sh, baby, here is your big sister come to see you.' My mother lifted my naughty little baby sister out of the cot, and my little sister stopped crying at once.

My mother said, 'Come and look.'

My little sister was wrapped up in a big woolly white shawl, and my mother undid the shawl and there was my little sister! When my mother put her down on the bed, my little sister began to cry again.

She was a little, little red baby,

crying and crying.

'Waah-waah, waah-waah,' – like that. Isn't it a nasty noise?

My little sister had tiny hands and tiny little feet. She went on crying and crying, and curling up her toes, and beating with her arms in a very cross way.

My mother said, 'She likes being lifted up and cuddled. She is a very good baby when she is being cuddled and fussed, but when I put her down she cries and cries. She is an artful pussy,' my mother said.

I was very sorry to see my little sister crying, and I was disappointed because I didn't want a crying little sister very much, but I went and looked at her. I looked at her little red face and her little screwed up eyes and her little crying mouth and then I said, 'Don't cry, baby, don't cry, baby.'

And, do you know, when I said, 'Don't cry, baby,' my little sister *stopped crying*, really stopped crying at once. For me! Because *I* told her to. She opened her eyes and she looked and looked and she didn't cry any more.

My mother said, 'Just fancy! She must know you are her own big sister! She has stopped crying.'

I was pleased to think that my little sister had stopped crying because she knew I was her big sister, and I put my finger on my sister's tiny, tiny hand and my little sister caught hold of my finger tight with her little curly fingers.

My mother said I could hold my little sister on my lap if I was careful. So I sat down on a chair and my godmother-aunt put my little sister on to my lap, and I held her very carefully; and my little sister didn't cry at all. She went to sleep like a good baby.

And do you know, she was so small and so sweet and she held my finger so tightly with her curly little fingers that I loved her and loved her and although she often cried after that I never minded it a bit, because I knew how nice and cuddly she could be when she was good!

2. My Naughty Little Sister
and the book-little-boy

Do you like having stories read to you?
When I was a little girl I used to like it
very much. My little sister liked it too,
but she pretended that she didn't.

When my sister and I were very little
children we had a kind aunt who used
to come and read stories to us. She used
to read all the stories that she'd had
read to her when *she* was a little girl.

I used to listen and listen and say,
'Go on! Go on!' whenever my auntie
stopped for a minute, but my little
sister used to pretend that she wasn't

listening. Wasn't she silly? She used to fidget with her old doll, Rosy-Primrose, and pretend that she was playing babies with her, but really she listened and listened too, and heard every word.

Do you know how I knew that she listened and listened? I'll tell you. When my little sister was in bed at night she used to tell the stories all over again to Rosy-Primrose.

One day when my aunt came to read to us, she said, 'I've got a book here that I won as a Sunday School prize. I used to like these stories when I was a child, I hope you will like them too.'

So our aunt read us a story about a poor little boy. It was a very sad story in the beginning because this poor little boy was very ragged and hungry. It said that he had no breakfast and no dinner and no supper, but it was lovely at the end because a nice kind lady took him home with her and said she was his real mother and gave him lots of nice things to eat and lots of nice clothes to wear, and a white pony. But the 'nothing to eat' part was very sad.

Now, you know, my little sister liked eating, and she was so surprised to hear about the book-little-boy with nothing to eat that she forgot to pretend that she wasn't listening and she said, 'No breakfast?' She said 'no breakfast' in a very little voice.

Our auntie said, 'No, no breakfast.'

My little sister said, 'No dinner?' She said that in a little voice too, because she thought no dinner and no breakfast was terrible.

My aunt said, 'No dinner, *and* no supper,' and she was so pleased to think that my funny little sister *had* been listening that she said, 'Would you like to see the picture?' And my little sister said 'please' and I said 'please' too.

So our kind aunt showed us the

picture in the book that went with the poor little boy story. It was a very miserable picture because the little boy was sitting all alone in the corner of a room, looking very sad. There was an empty plate on the floor beside this poor little boy, and under the picture it said, '*Nothing to eat*.'

Wasn't that sad?

My little sister thought it was very sad. She looked and looked at the picture and she said, '*No* breakfast, *no* dinner, and *no* supper.' Like that, over and over again.

My aunt said, 'Cheer up. He had lots to eat when his kind rich mother

took him home in the end; he had a
pony too, remember,' my aunt said.

But my sister said, 'No *picture*
dinner. Poor, poor boy,' she said.

Well now, when the reading time

was over my little sister was a very quiet child. She was very quiet when she had her supper. She sat by the fire and my mother gave her a big piece of buttery bread and a big mug of warm sweet milk, but she was very quiet, she said, 'thank you' in a tiny quiet voice, and she drank up her milk like a good child. When my mother came to say that the hot-water bottle was in her bed, she said her prayers at once and went straight upstairs.

My mother kissed my warm little sister and said 'good night' to her, and my little sister said 'good night'. But when my kind aunt kissed her and said, 'good night' to her, my little sister said, '*No* breakfast, *no* dinner,' and my auntie said, 'No supper,' but my little sister smiled and said, '*yes, supper*.' My little sister looked very smiley and pleased with herself.

When our aunt went to go home, and looked for the Sunday School prize-book, she knew why my little sister had said such a funny thing.

Do you know what that silly child had done? She had put her piece of buttery bread inside the Sunday School prize-book, on top of the little book boy's picture. She had given her supper to the book-little-boy!

Of course the book was very greasy and crumby after that, which was a pity because our aunt had kept it very tidy indeed as it had been a prize. I suppose it was a very naughty thing to have done.

But my little sister hadn't *meant* to be naughty. She thought that she had given the book-little-boy her own supper, and you know she was quite a greedy child, so it was a kind thing to do really.

Now you know why she said, '*No* breakfast, *no* dinner, and *yes, supper*,' don't you?

3. My Naughty Little Sister and poor Charlie Cocoa

In the days when I was a little girl, and my naughty little sister was a very small child, my little sister often helped Mrs Cocoa Jones to do her housework. Mrs Cocoa worked *so* hard, and had *such* a clean and tidy house, that she was glad when my little sister came to help her.

Mrs Cocoa Jones had a shiny red dustpan and a brush with a red handle, and because my little sister was such a helpful child, Mrs Cocoa bought her a nice little shiny red dustpan and a little brush with a red handle for herself. Wasn't that very kind of her?

Mrs Cocoa hung her dustpan and brush on a hook behind her broom-cupboard door when she wasn't using them, and dear Mr Cocoa put another hook behind the broom-cupboard door so that my little sister could hang her dustpan and brush there too. It was a nice low hook so that my little sister could reach it all by herself. What a smiley pleased girl she was when she saw her own little dustpan and brush hanging underneath Mrs Cocoa's big dustpan and brush!

'Now we shall *work* and *work*, Mrs Cocoa,' my little sister said.

When Mrs Cocoa swept her carpets, she knelt on the floor and brushed the dust into her dustpan, and my little sister knelt on the floor too, and brushed the dust into *her* dustpan. *Sweep sweep* went Mrs Cocoa's big brush and *sweep sweep* went my little sister's small brush. 'Aren't we busy, Mrs Cocoa?' said my little sister as she brushed and brushed.

Mrs Cocoa would sit up and say, 'Oh! My *poor* back!' and my naughty little sister would sit up and say, 'Oh, *my* poor back!' and then they would

carry their pans of dust out to the dustbin and grumble and grumble about hard work.

My little sister was only pretending to grumble, because she liked helping Mrs Cocoa and her back wasn't really bad at all, but poor Mrs Cocoa really was grumbling when she said, 'Oh my *poor* back!'

Now, kind Mr Cocoa was very worried about Mrs Cocoa's poor back, so one day he took some money out of his savings and bought Mrs Cocoa a fine vacuum cleaner.

Mrs Cocoa was pleased! She had never had a vacuum cleaner before, and when Mr Cocoa fixed it up for her, and showed her how quickly it worked, she was very excited.

Mrs Cocoa was so excited that she hurried out into her back-garden, and called to my little sister who was playing in our garden. 'Come and see what Mr Jones has bought for me!' she called and my little sister ran and fetched her dolly, Rosy-Primrose, to see too.

Then my little sister hurried through her very own little gate into Mr Cocoa's garden, then through the back door into Mrs Cocoa's shiny-clean kitchen. *Then my little sister stopped.* She stood still and *listened.*

There was a funny, humming noise coming from Mrs Cocoa's sitting-room, and my little sister didn't like it.

'Come in,' said Mrs Cocoa, 'come and see my new cleaner.'

Then my little sister walked

forward and looked in at the sitting-room door. She had never seen a vacuum cleaner before, so she stared and stared and listened and listened. And she didn't like it one bit!

'I don't like it!' said my naughty little sister. 'I want to go home!'

Then Mr Cocoa switched off the cleaner and the noise stopped, but my little sister still didn't like it. 'I want to go home,' she said.

'But it's to help poor Mrs Cocoa do her work,' said Mr Cocoa in his nice kind voice. 'It will eat all the nasty dust for her.'

'I help Mrs Cocoa do the work!'

said my sister. '*I* help Mrs Cocoa do the work!' and she began to cry, and cry, and she ran right out of Mrs Cocoa's tidy clean house and back to our house, crying and crying. *And she wouldn't go to see Mrs Cocoa at all.*

My little sister would not go into Mrs Cocoa's house for a long while, and, if she heard the cleaner working when she was playing in our garden she ran straight in to our mother and hid her face in our mother's apron, because she didn't like the noise the cleaner made.

Now Mrs Cocoa Jones was very very sad when my little sister wouldn't come to see her, because she loved my bad little sister very much. The vacuum cleaner did a lot of work for Mrs Cocoa, and her bad back was a good deal better, but Mrs Cocoa was still sad. So she spoke to Mr Cocoa, and he said he would have a word with my little sister and see if he could make her like the vacuum after all.

One morning when Mr Cocoa was digging his garden, and my little sister was blowing some of the lovely white fluffy seeds from a dandelion flower, Mr Cocoa said, 'I should think our Charlie would like some of that fluff.'

My little sister was surprised to

hear Mr Cocoa say this because she didn't know anything about Charlie.

'Poor Charlie gets so hungry,' said Mr Cocoa Jones, 'and all we can give him to eat is dust and dirt – and he does love some nice fluff if he can get it.'

'What Charlie?' said my little sister. 'What Charlie is hungry?'

'Charlie the cleaner,' said clever Mr Cocoa. 'Charlie who eats the dirt for Mrs Cocoa. There's not a lot of dirt in our house you know,' he said, 'poor old Charlie.'

Mr Cocoa spoke so nicely that Charlie sounded just like a poor hungry boy and my little sister felt quite sorry about him. So she gave Mr Cocoa the dandelion flower seeds and said, 'For Charlie,' and Mr Cocoa took them indoors.

Then my little sister heard the sound of Mrs Cocoa's cleaner, but this time she didn't run indoors, she stood and listened to the sound poor Charlie made when he ate the dandelion fluff and she was quite glad to think that she had given it to him.

When Mr Cocoa came out again, my little sister said, 'Did Charlie like it?' and Mr Cocoa said, 'Yes, it was a treat for him.' So then my little sister went up and down the garden and picked a lot of dandelion clocks for Charlie.

'Why don't you come and give them to him?' said Mr Cocoa. 'Come and see him eat them all up. Poor old Charlie,' Mr Cocoa said.

'Poor old Charlie,' said my little sister, and because she was quite sorry for poor Charlie, she went into Mrs Cocoa's house to see him.

When my little sister really looked at poor Charlie she wasn't a bit frightened. She saw that he had a round shiny body and a long trunk-thing. There was a shiny handle fixed to Charlie's trunk that had a black mouth-looking thing at the end of it.

'Hello, Charlie Cocoa,' said my little sister, 'you are a funny-looking boy.'

When Mr Cocoa switched on Charlie's noise, my little sister didn't like it at all, but she wasn't frightened any more. She laughed and put her hands over her ears, and watched as Charlie ate up all the dandelion seeds. He was hungry! My little sister knew that there *wouldn't* be very much for him on Mrs Cocoa's clean floors. She knew that you had to do a great deal of brushing to get even a little dust from those carpets.

My little sister was so sorry for

Charlie, that, can you ever guess what she did? She went to Mr Cocoa's broom cupboard, and got out her own little dustpan and brush, and then she went out into Mrs Cocoa's garden, and swept up a nice pan of dust from the path, and brought it in and gave it to him.

'There, Charlie, eat it up do,' my little sister said. 'Poor Charlie! Poor Charlie Cocoa!'

4. My Naughty Little Sister and the big girl's bed

A long time ago, when my naughty little sister was a very small girl, she had a nice cot with pull-up sides so that she couldn't fall out and bump herself.

My little sister's cot was a very pretty one. It was pink, and had pictures of fairies and bunny-rabbits painted on it.

It had been my old cot when I was a very small child and I had taken care of the pretty pictures. I used to kiss the fairies 'good night' when I went to bed, but my bad little sister did not kiss them and take care of their pictures. Oh no!

My naughty little sister did dreadful things to those poor fairies. She scribbled on them with pencils and scratched them with tin-lids, and knocked them with poor old Rosy-Primrose her doll, until there were hardly any pictures left at all. She said, 'Nasty fairies. Silly old rabbits.'

There! Wasn't she a bad child? You wouldn't do things like that, would you?

And my little sister jumped and jumped on her cot. After she had been tucked up at night-time she would get out from under the covers, and jump and jump. And when she woke up in the morning she jumped and jumped again, until one day, when she was jumping, the bottom fell right out of the cot, and my naughty little sister, and the mattress, and the covers, and poor Rosy-Primrose all fell out on to the floor!

Then our mother said, 'That child must have a bed!' Even though our father managed to mend the cot, our mother said, 'She must have a bed!'

My naughty little sister said, 'A big bed for me?'

And our mother said, 'I am afraid so, you bad child. You are too rough now for your poor old cot.'

My little sister wasn't ashamed of being too rough for her cot. She was pleased because she was going to have a new bed, and she said, 'A big girl's bed for me!'

My little sister told everybody that she was going to have a big girl's bed.

She told her kind friend the window-cleaner man, and the coalman, and the milkman. She told the dustman too. She said, 'You can have my old cot soon, dustman, because I am going to have a big girl's bed.' And she was as pleased as pleased.

But our mother wasn't pleased at all. She was rather worried. You see, our mother was afraid that my naughty little sister would jump and jump on her new bed, and scratch it, and treat it badly. My naughty little sister had done such dreadful things to her old cot, that my mother was afraid she would spoil the new bed too.

Well now, my little sister told the lady who lived next door all about her new bed. The lady who lived next door to us was called Mrs Jones, but my little sister used to call her Mrs Cocoa Jones because she used to go in and have a cup of cocoa with her every morning.

Mrs Cocoa Jones was a very kind lady, and when she heard about the new bed she said, 'I have a little yellow eiderdown and a yellow counterpane upstairs, and they are too small for any of my beds, so when your new bed comes, I will give them to you.'

My little sister was excited, but when

she told our mother what Mrs Cocoa had said, our mother shook her head.

'Oh, dear,' she said, 'what will happen to the lovely eiderdown and counterpane when our bad little girl has them?'

Then, a kind aunt who lived near us said, 'I have a dear little green nightie-case put away in a drawer. It belonged to me when I was a little girl. When your new bed comes you can have it to put your nighties in like a big girl.'

My little sister said, 'Good. Good,' because of all the nice things she was going to have for her bed. But our mother was more worried than ever.

She said, 'Oh dear! That pretty nightie-case. You'll spoil it, I know you will!'

But my little sister went on being pleased as pleased about it.

Then one day the new bed arrived. It was a lovely shiny brown bed, new as new, with a lovely blue stripy mattress to go on it: new as new. And there was a new stripy pillow too. Just like a real big girl would have.

My little sister watched while my mother took the poor old cot to pieces, and stood it up against the wall. She watched when the new bed was put up, and the new mattress was laid on top of it. She watched the new pillow being put into a clean white case, and when our mother made the bed with clean new sheets and clean new blankets, she said, 'Really big-girl! A big girl's bed – all for me.'

Then Mrs Cocoa Jones came in, and she was carrying the pretty yellow eiderdown and the yellow counterpane. They were very shiny and satiny like buttercup flowers, and when our mother put them on top of the new bed, they looked beautiful.

Then our kind aunt came down the road, and *she* was carrying a little parcel, and in the little parcel was the pretty green nightie-case. My little sister ran down the road to meet her because she was so excited. She was more excited still when our aunt picked up her little nightdress and put it into the pretty green case and laid the green case on the yellow shiny eiderdown.

My little sister was so pleased that

she was glad when bedtime came.

And, what do you think? She got carefully, carefully into bed with Rosy-Primrose, and she laid herself down and stretched herself out – carefully, carefully like a good, nice girl.

And she didn't jump and jump, and she didn't scratch the shiny brown wood, or scribble with pencils or scrape with tin-lids. Not ever! Not even when she had had the new bed a long, long time.

My little sister took great care of her big girl's bed. She took great care of her shiny yellow eiderdown and counterpane and her pretty green nightie-case.

And whatever do you think she said
to me?

She said, 'You had the fairy pink
cot before I did. But this is my very
own big girl's bed, and I am going to
take great care
of my very
own bed, like
a big girl!'

5. The cross photograph

A long time ago, when I was a little girl with a naughty little sister who was younger than myself, our mother made us a beautiful coat each.

They were lovely red coats with black buttons to do them up with and curly-curly black fur on them to keep us warm. We were very proud children when we put our new red coats on.

Our mother was proud too, because she had never made any coats before, and she said, 'I know! You shall have your photographs taken. Then we can always remember how smart they look.'

So our proud mother took my naughty little sister and me to have our photographs taken in our smart red coats.

The man in the photographer's shop was very smart too. He had curly-curly black hair *just* like the fur on our new coats, and he had a pink flower in his buttonhole and a yellow handkerchief that he waved and waved when he took our photographs.

There were lots of pictures in the shop. There were pictures of children, and ladies being married, and ladies smiling, and gentlemen smiling, and pussy-cats with long fur, and black-and-white rabbits. All those pictures! And the smart curly-curly man had taken every one himself!

He said we could go and look at his pictures while he talked to our mother, so I went round and looked at them. But do you know, my naughty little sister wouldn't look. She stood still as still and quiet as quiet, and she shut her eyes.

Yes, she did. She shut her eyes and wouldn't look at anything. She was being a stubborn girl, and when the photographer-man said, 'Are you both ready?' my bad little sister kept her eyes shut and said, '*No.*'

Our mother said, 'But surely you want your photograph taken?'

But my naughty little sister kept her eyes shut tight as tight, and said, 'No taken! No taken!' And she got so cross, and shouted so much, that the curly man said, 'All right then. I will just take your big sister by herself.'

'I will take a nice photograph of your big sister,' said the photographer-man, 'and she will be able to show it to all her friends. Wouldn't you like a photograph of yourself to show to your friends?'

My naughty little sister did want a

photograph of herself to show to her friends, but she would not say so. She just said, 'No photograph!'

So our mother said, 'Oh well, it looks as if it will be only one picture then, for we can't keep this gentleman waiting all day.'

So the photographer-man made me stand on a box-thing. There was a little table on the box-thing, and I had to put my hand on the little table and stand up straight and smile.

There was a beautiful picture of a garden on the wall behind me. It was such a big picture that when the photograph was taken it looked just as if I was standing in a real garden. Wasn't that a clever idea?

When I was standing quite straight and quite smiley, the curly photographer-man shone a lot of bright lights, and then he got his big black camera-on-legs and said, 'Watch for the dickey-bird!' And he waved and waved his yellow handkerchief. And then 'click!' said the camera, and my picture was safe inside it.

'That's all,' said the man, and he helped me to get down.

Now, what do you think? While the man was taking my picture, my little sister had opened her eyes to peep, and when she saw me standing all straight and smiley in my beautiful new coat, and heard the man say, 'Watch for the dickey-bird,' and saw him wave his yellow handkerchief, she stared and stared.

The man said, 'That was all right, wasn't it?' and I said, 'Yes, thank you.'

Then the curly man looked at my little sister and he saw that her eyes weren't shut any more so he said, 'Are you going to change your mind now?'

And what do you think? My little sister changed her mind. She stopped being stubborn. She changed her mind and said, 'Yes, please,' like a good polite child. You see, she hadn't known anything about photographs before, and she had been frightened, but when she saw me having my picture taken, and had seen how easy it was, she hadn't been frightened any more.

She let the man lift her on to the box-thing. She was so small though, that he took the table away and found a little chair for her to sit on, and gave her a teddy-bear to hold.

Then he said, 'Smile nicely now,' and my naughty little sister smiled very beautifully indeed.

The man said, 'Watch for the dickey-bird,' and he waved his yellow handkerchief to her, and 'click', my naughty little sister's photograph had been taken too!

But what do you think? *She hadn't kept smiling*. When the photographs came home for us to look at, there was my little sister holding the teddy-bear and looking as cross as cross.

Our mother *was* surprised, she said, 'I thought the man told you to *smile*!'

And what do think that funny girl said? She said, 'I did smile, but there wasn't any dickey-bird, so I stopped.'

My mother said, 'Oh dear! We shall have to have it taken all over again!'

But our father said, 'No, I like this one. It is such a natural picture. I like it as it is.' And he laughed and laughed and laughed and laughed.

My little sister liked the cross picture very much too, and sometimes, when she hadn't anything else to do, she climbed up to the looking-glass and made cross faces at herself. *Just* like the cross face in the photograph!

6. My Naughty Little Sister
wins a prize

A long time ago, when I was a little girl, my naughty little sister, who was smaller than me, had a lot of friends, but her favourite friends were the nice coalman, and the nice milkman, and the baker with a poor bad leg, and the window-cleaner man, and her very, very favourite friend was called Mr Blakey and he had a shoe-mending shop, and had rather a cross and roary voice.

Now one day everyone where we lived became very excited, because they heard that the town was going to have a Grand Carnival.

Everyone talked and talked about the Carnival because the town had never had a Carnival before, and there were pictures of funny clowns with writing underneath in all the shop windows and stuck up on all the fences. The clown was to show how jolly and funny the Grand Carnival was going to be, and the writing was to tell about all the nice things that would be happening when Carnival Day came.

My little sister liked the clown-picture very much, and because she wasn't old enough to read, she asked our mother to tell her what the writing was about, and she asked questions and questions.

My mother told her that all the shops would be shut and there would be swings and roundabouts in the park, and a band.

My little sister asked more questions and questions, and my father told her that there would be pony-rides and toe-dancing and fireworks and a flower-show.

But my little sister still asked questions and questions until at last our father and mother said, 'You must wait and see for yourself when Carnival Day comes.'

Well now, there was one thing about the Grand Carnival that my little sister liked to hear best of all, and that was the Grand Procession and Fancy Dress Parade.

Do you know what that means? It means that lots of people dress up in beautiful clothes or funny clothes and they go through all the streets of the town so that everyone can see them. Some of the people walk, and some ride in cars or on lorries or bicycles, and the people who look the most beautiful or the funniest, win prizes.

Do you know why my little sister was so interested in the Grand Procession and Fancy Dress Parade? It was because all her special friends were going to be in it.

When the nice coalman came, he told my naughty little sister that he was going to wash down the coal-cart and put lovely red ribbons on his horse, and that all the Infant School children were going to ride with him. He said that the Infant School children were going to be dressed up as fairies and pixies. The nice coalman said that *he* wasn't going to be a fairy or a pixie, but that he was going to wear his Sunday-best hat, so, of course, my little sister wanted to see him very much.

The nice milkman said he was going to have lots of flags on his cart, and that all the pretty ladies from the dairy shop were going to be dressed up to look like milkmaids, and walk beside it with milking pails. The milkman said that he was going to be dressed up, too.

When my little sister asked the milkman what he was going to be dressed up *as*, the milkman said, 'Ah! Just you wait and see! I'll be very fancy, I promise you!'

That sounded so exciting that my little sister wanted to see *him* very much indeed.

The nice baker said that he was going to leave his cart at home because he was going to march *with his medals up* with the other old soldiers. That did sound grand – 'march with his medals up'.

My little sister could hardly wait to see the nice baker marching with his poor bad leg along with all the other old soldiers, and she told the nice baker that she would keep a very special look-out for *him*.

When the window-cleaner man

came, he said that he was going to dress his barrow up with roses and roses, and that his little niece was going to be a rose-fairy on the top. Didn't that sound pretty? My little sister thought it did, and she said, 'I wish the Grand Carnival Day would hurry up!'

My little sister was so pleased and so excited about the Carnival that she went in to see her dear friend Mr Blakey at the shoe-mending shop to see what *he* was going to dress up as.

But Mr Blakey said he was too old for dressing up and being a poppy-show. He said that if everyone dressed

up and walked in the Grand
Procession there wouldn't be anyone
to watch it, and then there would
be no reason for dressing up at all.
Mr Blakey said he was going to be
a spectator.

My naughty little sister did not
know what 'spectator' meant so Mr

Blakey said it meant someone who looked on.

So my little sister said, 'I will be a Spectator too, and Mother will be a Spectator, and Father will be a Spectator, and my big sister will be a Spectator.' And she was very pleased indeed.

But my naughty little sister wasn't a spectator. No, she was *something else*.

This is what happened.

The day before the Grand Carnival Day, the window-cleaner man came to our house. He didn't bring his barrow, he came on a bicycle and looked very worried.

The window-cleaner man told my mother that his little niece was not a well girl, and that she had got to stay in bed for a few days. He said she wouldn't be able to be the rose-fairy on his barrow after all, and he asked my mother if she would let my little sister ride on his barrow instead. He said that my little sister was just the same size as his little niece, so that the rose-fairy frock would fit her nicely.

Wasn't that a lovely idea? It was very sad about the poor little not-well niece wasn't it? But it was lovely for my naughty little sister.

My little sister said, 'Please let me,

please. *Please* do.'

My mother said, 'I don't know. You do get into such dreadful mischief.'

But the window-cleaner man said, 'She can't come to any harm on the barrow.'

And my little sister said, 'I will be good – I will be very, very good. I *promise*.'

So at last my mother said, 'Well, if it's a fine day tomorrow, she may go.'

The window-cleaner man and my little sister were both very pleased when our mother said this, and they were more pleased still next morning, when they saw the bright sunshine, and knew that it was going to be a fine day.

So, my little sister was dressed up in the beautiful rose-fairy dress that the poor little ill niece had been going to wear, and it was a perfect fit.

The rose-fairy dress was pink, and sticking out, and it had dear little green wings – just like leaves.

When my little sister was dressed she ran through her own little gate in the back-garden to see Mr and Mrs Cocoa Jones who lived next door, to show them how smart she was, and Mrs Cocoa said that she looked just like a real fairy.

My naughty little sister was so pleased that she danced a special little made-up dance for them. She would have danced for a long time, only my mother called, 'Hurry up, or the Parade will start without you.'

So my little sister went off with my mother through the town to the place that the procession was to start from, and everyone stared as they went by, to see such a very pretty rose-fairy in the street, and my little sister held tight to Mother's hand and looked very pleased and smiley. She was a proud girl!

She was prouder still when she saw the window-cleaning barrow, because it looked so beautiful. It was covered with so many beautiful roses that you couldn't see that it was a barrow at all, and there was a dear little chair made of roses for my little sister to sit on, and a sunshade of rose-petals for her to hold.

(They weren't real roses, of course – they were made of paper, but they looked *very* real. I thought you would be wondering about the prickles if I didn't explain this.)

The window-cleaner man had a smart white coat on, and a new straw hat, with a rose in his button-hole, and he was very glad to see how pretty my sister looked. 'You are a credit to your family,' he said to her, and he lifted her up very carefully into the little chair, and our mother spread out her sticking-out skirt, and tidied her wings and made her look really lovely.

While she was waiting for the parade to start, she looked at all the other fancy-dressed people, and they were all very lovely too. She saw her friend the coalman with his cart. He looked very clean and nice – not a bit coaly today, and his cart had lots of tree-branches tied all over it, and all the Infant School children were in the cart, laughing and shouting, and waving their fairy wands. The coalman didn't see my little sister, because he was walking along beside the horse, but she saw him and his Sunday best hat, too.

My little sister saw her friend the milkman as well, although he looked so funny that she hardly knew him, but she knew his cart, and she knew the young ladies from the shop – even though they were all dressed up as milkmaids! The milkman had a tall black hat like a chimney-pot, and his nose was painted red, and he looked a little bit like the clown on the Grand Carnival pictures. The milkman saw my little sister and he waved to her. But my little sister didn't wave back, she sat still and quiet, because she wanted to be good today.

She didn't see the baker because all the Old Soldiers were walking at the front of the parade, behind the band, but she saw lots of other old soldiers with their medals up, and they all looked so smart and nice, and their medals were so shiny, that she knew the poor bad-leg baker must be looking very grand indeed.

Then the band began to play, and the procession started. The window-cleaner man said, 'Ups-adaisy', and

he took up the handles of his barrow –
that you couldn't see for roses and
roses – and off they went, and
everyone saw my pretty little rose-
fairy sister, with her dress spread
out nicely, and her leafy little wings
sticking up quite straight – looking as
good as gold.

Mr Blakey hadn't known that my
little sister was going to be in the
procession, and he *was* surprised when
he saw her going by. He waved and
waved, and said, 'Bravo-hooray,' until
my little sister saw him. When she did,
she waved to him and blew him a little
kiss, and then she sat good and still

again, while the window-cleaner man
pushed and pushed.

And what do you think? When the
Grand Procession and Fancy Dress
Parade was over, the window-cleaner
man got a first prize for his beautiful
rose barrow. And my little sister was

given a special prize for looking so beautiful and being so good.

The window-cleaner man had a little wooden clock for his prize, and my little sister had a baby doll with shutting eyes and a long white dress.

The window-cleaner man said that my little sister had been a thoroughly good child, and when my little sister thanked him for taking her, he said it was a treat to have her with him.

Then she did a kind and generous thing, she did it all her own self, without anyone telling her to. My little sister remembered that poor ill little niece who couldn't wear the nice dress or go in the parade – so she gave the shutting-eye doll to the window-cleaner man and asked him to give it to his poor ill niece, who couldn't be in the procession. Wasn't that nice of her?

My little sister said she was very, very sorry about the ill little niece, but that she was very glad all the same to have been in the Grand Procession.

The window-cleaner man said that next time there was a Carnival, he would put two little chairs on his barrow, and then my little sister and his little niece could be fairies together.

7. My Naughty Little Sister and the baby

One day, long ago, when I was a little girl and my naughty little sister was a very little girl, a lady called Mrs Rogers asked my mother if she would mind her little boy-baby for the afternoon.

My mother was very pleased to help Mrs Rogers. 'I should be glad to mind the baby,' she said.

I was very pleased to think we were going to have a little boy-baby in our house for a whole afternoon, but my little sister said, 'I don't know babies, do I?'

Our mother said, 'No, but I expect you will know this one quite well by the time Mrs Rogers comes for it. You can't help knowing babies,' our mother said.

And my little sister said, 'Well, I hope I am glad when I know it.'

Well now, when Mrs Rogers came, my silly sister would not go out to look at the baby, she stood at the door and behaved in a very shy and peepy way and waited for our mother to call her.

'Come and look at the boy-baby,' said Mother, and she took my sister by the hand to look at the baby in the pram.

He was a very dear baby. He was kicking and cooing and smiling and looking very happy.

'Isn't he nice?' my mother said.

My little sister didn't say, 'Yes, he is nice,' because she didn't know the baby very well then, she said, 'He's very fat.'

My mother told my little sister, 'All babies are fat. *You* were fat too,' she said.

My little sister was very surprised to hear that she had been fat like the boy-baby. She stuck out her tummy and blew out her cheeks to look fat, and said, 'Fat girl.'

When the baby saw my little sister pretending to be fat, he began to laugh, and when he laughed he showed a little white tooth. 'Look, a toothy,' said my little sister, and when she said, 'Look, a toothy', that little boy-baby laughed very loudly indeed, and he took off his white woolly cap and he threw it right out of the pram!

My little sister picked up the white woolly cap for the baby.

'Put it back on his head,' our mother said, and my little sister did put it back on his head, and do you know, the bad boy-baby pulled his cap straight off again and threw it out of the pram!

So – my little sister picked the cap up *again* – and put it on the boy-baby's head *again*, and that naughty boy pulled it off and threw it away and laughed and laughed, and my little sister laughed as well because the boy-baby was so jolly and so fat.

Then my little sister talked to the baby, 'You must keep your cap *on*,' she said, and she pulled it on very carefully and tightly, and when he tried to pull it off again it only fell over one of his eyes.

Then my little sister put his cap straight, and *then* she did a very clever thing to make him forget all about his cap. She popped her old doll, Rosy-Primrose, round the side of the pram, and said, 'Boh!' And the boy-baby was so pleased he giggled and giggled.

So my little sister popped Rosy-Primrose round the pram again and again, and each time the funny baby giggled and my little sister giggled. Mother laughed and I laughed too to see my funny sister and the funny boy-baby.

Then my little sister said to the boy-baby, 'What is your name?' and the boy-baby laughed again and said, 'Ay-ay.'

'Where do you live?' asked my little sister, and the boy-baby said, 'Ay-ay' again. Then the baby said, 'Oigle, oigle, oigle,' and my sister said, 'That's a funny thing to say.'

My mother said, 'He doesn't talk properly yet. *You* didn't talk when you were a baby.'

What a surprise for my naughty little sister. 'Not talk!'

When tea-time came the baby sat in

the old high-chair next to my naughty little sister, and my mother gave him some crusts with butter on them.

That bad baby dropped some of his crusts on the floor, and sucked some of them, and waved some of them about, and then he tried to push a crust into my little sister's ear. She was cross!

But our mother told her that the

baby was too little to know any better, so my little sister forgave the baby and laughed at him.

When tea was over, the baby lay in his pram and played with his toes, and then he fell asleep. He was fast asleep when Mrs Rogers came to take him home.

When my naughty little sister went to bed that night, do you know what she did? She pretended that she couldn't talk, she said, 'Ay-ay, ay-ay,' and played with her toes just like the boy-baby did.

Then she *did* speak, she said, 'I know lots about babies now, don't I?'

8. Bad Harry's haircut

Quite a long time ago, when I was a little girl, my naughty little sister used to play with a little boy called Harry.

This boy Harry only lived a little way away from us, and as there were no nasty roads to cross between our houses, Harry used to come all on his own to play with my little sister, and she used to go all on her own to play with him. And they were Very Good Friends.

And they were both very naughty children. Oh dear!

But, if you could have seen this Bad Harry you wouldn't have said that he was a naughty child. He looked so very good. Yes, he looked very good indeed.

My little sister never looked very good, even when she was behaving herself, but Bad Harry looked good all the time.

My naughty little sister's friend Harry had big, big blue eyes and pretty golden curls like a baby angel, but oh dear, he was quite naughty all the same.

Now one day, when my little sister went round to play with Harry she found him looking very smart indeed. He was wearing real big boy's trousers. Real ones, with real big boy's buttons and real big boy's braces. Red braces like a very big boy! Wasn't he smart?

'Look,' said Bad Harry, 'look at my big boy's trousers.'

'Smart,' said my naughty little sister, 'smart boy.'

'I'm going to have a real boy's haircut too,' said Bad Harry. 'Today.

Not Mummy with scissors any more; but a real boy's haircut in a real barber's shop!'

My word, he was a proud boy!

My little sister was *so* surprised, and Bad Harry was so pleased to see how surprised she was.

'I'll be a big boy then,' he said.

Then Harry's mother, who was a kind lady and liked my little sister very much, said that if she was a good girl she could come to the barber's and see Harry have his hair cut.

My little sister was so excited that she ran straight back home at once to tell our mother all about Harry's big boy's trousers and Harry's real boy's haircut. 'Can I go too, can I go too?' she asked our mother.

Our mother said, 'Yes, you may go, only hold very tight to Harry's mother's hand when you cross the High Street,' and my little sister promised that she would hold very tight indeed.

So off they went to the barber's to get Harry a Real Boy's Haircut.

My little sister had never been in a barber's shop before and she stared and stared. Bad Harry had never been in a barber's shop before either, but he didn't stare, he pretended that he knew all about it, he picked up one of the barber's books and pretended to look at the pictures in it, but he peeped all the time at the barber's shop.

There were three haircut-men in the barber's shop, and they all had white coats and they all had black combs sticking out of their pockets.

There were three white wash-basins with shiny taps and looking-glasses, and three very funny chairs. In the three funny chairs were three men all having something done to them by the three haircut-men.

One man was having his hair cut with scissors, and one man was having his neck clipped with clippers, and one man had a soapy white face and *he* was being shaved!

And there were bottles and bottles, and brushes and brushes, and towels and towels, and pretty pictures with writing on them, and all sorts of things to see! My little sister looked and Bad Harry peeped until it was Harry's turn to have his hair cut.

When it was Harry's turn one of the haircut-men fetched a special high-chair for Harry to sit in, because the grown-up chairs were all too big.

Harry sat in the special chair and then the haircut-man got a big blue sheet and wrapped it round Harry and tucked it in at the neck. 'You don't want any tickly old hairs going down there,' the haircut-man said.

Then the haircut man took his sharp shiny scissors and began to cut and cut. And down fell a golden curl and 'Gone!' said my little sister, and down fell another golden curl and 'Gone!' said my little sister again, and she said, 'Gone!' 'Gone!' 'Gone!' all the time until Harry's curls had quite gone away. Then she said, 'All gone now!'

When the haircut-man had finished cutting he took a bottle with a squeezer-thing and he squirted some nice smelly stuff all over Harry's head, and made Harry laugh, and my little sister laughed as well.

Then the haircut man took the big black comb, and he made a Big Boy's Parting on Harry's head, and he combed Harry's hair back into a real boy's haircut and then Bad Harry climbed down from the high-chair so that my little sister could really look at him.

And then my little sister *did* stare. Bad Harry's mother stared too . . .

For there was that bad boy Harry, with his real boy's trousers and his real boy's braces, with a real boy's haircut, smiling and smiling, and looking very pleased.

'No curls now,' said Bad Harry. 'Not any more.'

'No curls,' said my

naughty little sister.

'No,' Bad Harry's mother said, 'and oh dear, you don't even *look* good any more.'

Then my little sister laughed and laughed.

'Bad Harry!' she said. 'Bad Harry. All bad now – like me!'

9. My Naughty Little Sister shows off

Do you like climbing? My naughty little sister used to like climbing very much indeed. She climbed up fences and on chairs and down ditches and round railings, and my mother used to say, 'One day that child will fall and hurt herself.'

But our father said, 'She will be all right if she is careful.'

And my little sister *was* careful. She didn't want to hurt herself. She climbed on *easy things*, and when she knew she had gone far enough, she always came down again, slowly, slowly, carefully, carefully – one foot down – the other foot down – like that.

My little sister was so careful about climbing that our father nailed a piece of wood on to our front gate, so that she would have something to stand on when she wanted to look over it. There was a tree by the gate, and Father put an iron handle on the tree to help her to hold on tight. Wasn't he a kind daddy?

Well now, one day my naughty little sister went down to the front gate because she thought it would be nice to see all the people going by.

She climbed up carefully, carefully, like a good girl, and she held on to the iron handle, and she watched all the people going down the street.

First the postman came along. He said, 'Hello, Monkey,' and that made her laugh. She said, 'Hello, postman, have you any letters for this house?' and the postman said, 'Not today I'm afraid, Monkey.'

My little sister laughed again because the postman called her 'Monkey', but she remembered to hold on tight.

Then Mr Cocoa Jones went by on his bicycle. Mr Cocoa said, 'Don't fall,' and he ling-alinged his bicycle bell at her. 'Be very careful,' said Mr Cocoa Jones, and 'ling-aling', said Mr Cocoa Jones's bell.

My naughty little sister said, 'I won't fall. I won't fall, Mr Cocoa. I'm sensible,' and Mr Cocoa ling-a-linged

his bell again and
called 'Good-bye'.

My naughty little
sister waved to
Mr Cocoa. She
waved very
carefully. She
didn't lean forward to see him go
round the corner or anything silly like
that. No, she was most careful.

She was careful when the nice baker
came with the bread. She climbed
down, carefully, carefully and let him in.

She was careful when cars went by.
She held tight and stood very still. She
saw a steam-roller and a rag-a'-bone

man, and she held very tight indeed.

Then my naughty little sister saw her friend, Bad Harry, coming down the road, and she forgot to be sensible. She began to show off.

My little sister shouted, 'Harry, Harry, look at me. I'm on the gate, Harry.'

Bad Harry did look at her, because she called in such a loud voice, 'Look at me!' like that.

Then my silly little sister stood on one leg only – just because she wanted Bad Harry to think she was a clever girl.

That made Bad Harry laugh, so my little sister showed off again. She stood on the other leg only, and then – *she let go of the tree and waved her arms.*

And then – she fell right off the gate. Bump! She fell down and bumped her head.

Oh dear! Her head *did* hurt, and my poor little sister cried and cried. Bad Harry cried too, and my mother came hurrying out of the house to see what had happened.

Our dear mother said, 'Don't cry, don't cry, baby,' in a kind, kind voice. 'Don't cry, baby dear,' she said, and she picked my little sister up and took her indoors and Bad Harry followed them. They were still crying and crying.

They cried so much that my mother gave them each a sugar lump to suck. Then they stopped crying because they found that they couldn't cry and suck at the same time.

Then our mother looked at my little sister's poor head. 'What a nasty bruise,' our mother said. 'I think I had better put something on it for you, and you must be a good brave girl while I do it.'

My little sister was a good brave girl, too. She held Bad Harry's hand very tight, and she shut her eyes while

Mother put some stingy stuff out of a bottle on to her poor head. Our mother did it very quickly, and my brave sister didn't fidget and she didn't cry. Wasn't she good?

When our mother had finished she gave my little sister and her friend, Bad Harry, an apple each and they went into the garden to play.

They had a lovely time playing in the garden. First they picked

dandelions and put them in the water-
tub for boats. Then they played hide-
and-seek among the cabbages. Then
they made a little house underneath
the apple-tree. Then they found some
blue chalk and drew funny old men on
the tool-shed door.

And my little sister forgot all about
her poor head.

When our father came home and
saw my naughty little sister playing in
the garden he said, 'Hello, old lady,
have you been in the wars?' and my
little sister was surprised because she
had forgotten all about falling off the
gate. Father said, 'You have got a

nasty lump on top!'

So my little sister thought she would go indoors and look at her nasty lump. She climbed up on to a chair to look at herself in the mirror on the kitchen wall, and she saw that there was a big bump on her forehead. It was all yellowy-greeny.

Our mother said, 'Climbing again! I should think you would have had enough climbing for one day!'

My little sister looked at her big bump in the mirror, and then she climbed down from the chair, carefully, carefully.

She climbed down very carefully

indeed, and do you know what she said? She said, 'I like climbing very much, but I don't like falling down. And I *certainly* don't like nasty bumps on my head. So I don't think I will be a showing-off girl any more.'

10. My Naughty Little Sister
and the solid silver watch

A long time ago, when I was a little girl and my naughty little sister was very small, we had a dear old grandfather. Our dear old grandfather lived very near to us, and sometimes he came to our house, and sometimes we went to visit him.

When our grandfather came to see us, he wore very beautiful black clothes and a very smart black hat, and my little sister would say, 'Smart Grandad,' because he looked so nice.

Our grandfather told my little sister

that these smart clothes were his Sunday Blacks. He said he wore his Sunday Blacks when he went to church and when he went visiting, because they were his best clothes.

When our grandfather came to our house in his smart Sunday Blacks, he always sat down very carefully. He would put a big white handkerchief on his knees, and then lift my little sister up and let her sit on the big white handkerchief. But my little sister had to hold her legs out very carefully so that she wouldn't brush her dusty shoes on our grandfather's best Sunday Black trousers.

But when we went to see our grandfather in his house, he didn't wear his Sunday Blacks at all. He wore nice brown velvety trousers, with straps under his knees, and a soft furry waistcoat. He had a lovely red and white handkerchief too, but he didn't put that on his knees for my little sister to sit on.

Oh no. Grandfather didn't mind my little sister's dirty shoes when he was wearing his velvety trousers. He would let her climb up on to his lap all on her own and didn't mind how dirty her shoes were.

When my little sister sat on our

grandfather's lap, she always rubbed her face against his waistcoat. If she rubbed her face against his Sunday Black waistcoat, she rubbed it very, very carefully. But when we were at Grandfather's house she rubbed very hard against his soft furry one.

One day, when we were at our grandfather's house, and my naughty little sister was sitting on Grandfather's lap, she said a funny thing, she said:

'Grandad, I like your fur waistcoat better than your smart Sunday Black one. It smells tobacco-y. Your Sunday one smells mothball-y. I like tobacco better than mothball I think.'

Our grandfather laughed a lot and said he liked tobacco better than mothball too.

Then my little sister said, 'Your Sunday waistcoat and your furry waistcoat both talk *nick-nock, nick-nock*. Why do they both talk *nick-nock*, Grandad?'

Our grandfather didn't know what she meant about *nick-nock*, so he looked at my little sister very hard. Then he smiled and said, 'Of course, duckie, you mean my watch!'

Then our grandfather showed my little sister a thin leather strap that was on his waistcoat button and he said,

'Pull the strap, and you'll see who it is that says *nick-nock* – it isn't my waistcoat that says it at all.'

So my funny little sister pulled the thin leather strap. She pulled very slowly, and very carefully, because she was a little bit frightened, but when she had pulled enough out came a round silver box-thing with a round silver lid on it.

Our grandfather opened the round silver lid and there was a face just like the face on all the clocks everywhere.

'That's my watch,' our grandfather told my little sister. 'That is my solid silver watch. My old father had it once, and one day your father will have it. It is a very nice watch,' our grandfather said, 'it is *solid* silver.'

My little sister held the solid silver watch very carefully and looked at its round white face and the black clockhands and the little round silver lid. Then my little sister put the solid silver watch against her ear and listened to it saying *nick-nock, nick-nock, nick-nock*, over and over again.

My little sister liked the watch so much that she held it all the time. Very carefully, like a good child, my little sister held the solid silver watch.

When it was time to go, our mother

said, 'You must give the watch back to
Grandad now, so that he can put it in

his pocket again,' and my naughty little sister began to look cross, because she *did* like the solid silver watch so much.

But our grandfather said, 'I will let you put him back to bed for me, duckie, then he will be quite safe until you see me again.'

So then my little sister stopped being a cross girl and put the solid silver watch back into our grandfather's pocket her own self.

She said, 'I don't think I should like to go to bed in your pocket, Grandad. But the solid silver watch does. He still says *nick-nock*, doesn't he?'

After that my naughty little sister always asked to see the solid silver watch when she was with our grandfather, and he always let her hold it and listen to it say *nick-nock*.

And do you know, one evening, when our father and mother had to go out, our dear old grandfather came to look after us, and because my little sister was such a good girl, and went to bed so quietly, and said her prayers so nicely, our grandfather put his solid silver watch under her pillow, so that she could hear it say *nick-nock nick-nock* until she fell asleep.

11. Mrs Cocoa's white visitor

One cold and frosty morning, when I was a little girl and my sister was a very little girl, our mother and Mrs Jones next door and all the ladies living near us did lots and lots of washing and pegged it out on their clothes-lines.

There was a lot of hard cold snow on the ground, and there was a cold wind blowing, and my little sister was kneeling by the kitchen window watching Mother's washing and Mrs Cocoa Jones's washing and all

the other ladies' washing blowing
and blowing, and she laughed and
laughed.

My sister was laughing because all
the washing was frozen. The wind had
blown it, and the frost had frozen it
into funny shapes. Mother's big sheets

had gone all pointy-looking, and the tea-towels were sticking right up in the air. Mr Jones's woollies and socks looked hard and cold with icy teardrops hanging on them.

As for my sister's own little knickers and petticoats, the wind had blown them out into funny little balloons, and the frost had frozen them into funny little balloons, and they bobbed and bobbed on the line.

No wonder my sister laughed at the washing.

The wind blew 'whoo-oo' – like that – and the washing went 'snap-crack' on the line because it was so frozen.

'Will they stay like that now?' my sister said. 'Will they always be hard and funny-looking?'

'Oh no,' Mother told her. 'The sun will thaw them, and the wind will blow the water out of the clothes, and they will be quite soft again.'

'I am very glad about that,' said my little sister. 'I shouldn't like balloony knickers very much!'

And she went back to the window to see if the wind had blown them soft yet. She looked at all the whiteness. The cold snow white and the cold sheet white. All cold and white.

Then suddenly my sister shouted

and shouted, 'Mother, look, look!' she said. 'A big white washing-thing fell out of the sky on to Mrs Cocoa's garden.'

Mother said, 'Good gracious,' and looked out of the window, but she couldn't see anything.

But my sister jumped and jumped on the window-seat she was so excited. 'It fell down, it fell down,' she said, and jumped and jumped.

'You'll fall down too, if you aren't careful,' our mother said.

'I saw it, I saw it,' said my naughty little sister in a cross voice because she thought my mother wasn't being interested. 'It was all white and sheety-looking.'

And she might have shown off and been very cross indeed, only just then we heard Mrs Cocoa calling and calling, and we all ran out into the cold and frosty garden without thinking about our coats even, for dear Mrs Cocoa was saying, 'Help, help!'

Oh yes. My little sister *had* seen something come out of the sky; but it wasn't washing, and I don't think it really fell, but it must have looked as if it did.

It was a great white bird. A great white bird, with a long long neck and a black and yellow beak. It had come down into Mrs Cocoa Jones's garden, and Mrs Cocoa was saying, 'Help, help.'

Poor Mrs Cocoa had been hanging out some sheets when the bird came down and it had given her a fright. That was why she had shouted like that.

'Why,' said Mother, 'it's a swan!'

And so it was. My sister knew swans; she had seen them in the park. Sometimes we had gone to take bread to them. So now she had a good idea. She said, 'Give him some bread, Mrs Cocoa.'

Mrs Cocoa stopped being frightened. She said, 'What a clever girl you are,' and she hurried indoors to find a big piece of bread for the swan.

That was just what the swan wanted. He turned down his bendy head, and snapped with his black and yellow beak, and he swallowed up the piece of bread at once.

Our mother told us to go indoors and put our coats on, and while we did this, she found some stale bread for us to give the swan.

When Mrs Jones saw the swan eating bread in her snowy garden she became quite pleased and smiley, because swans don't often come into gardens, and some of the ladies from the other houses were beginning to look over their fences and say, 'Fancy that!' and 'Look – in Mrs Jones's garden – there's a swan!' It made dear Mrs Cocoa quite famous. It made my sister feel famous too because she had seen the swan first!

That swan was a very greedy bird. It wanted more and more to eat. Mrs Cocoa was glad when Mr Cocoa Jones came home on his bicycle for his dinner.

When Mr Cocoa saw the swan he said, 'That old fellow comes from the park. He's been out before.'

Then he said that the pond in the park was frozen hard, and he expected the swan had decided to fly away and look for a warmer place. Mr Cocoa said the swan couldn't fly far though, because the park swans had had something done to their wings to stop them going too far and becoming nuisances.

'It's a wonder it got as far as this,' Mr Jones said.

My sister asked Mr Cocoa if he was going to keep the swan now, but Mr Cocoa Jones was very shocked. 'Good gracious, no,' he said. 'That bird is *Crown Property*.'

He said that a man with a funny name would have to come and collect it.

My sister told me what Mr Jones

said, and she told me the man's funny name, she said, 'Mr Jones says he is going to stop at the Speeseeay man's house on his way back to work and ask him to fetch the swan.'

And she talked about the swan and the Speeseeay man all the time she was eating her dinner.

Presently two men came to Mrs Cocoa's house with a little green van. They said they knew the swan very well indeed; they said he was a 'bit of a rover'.

Then they asked everyone to go indoors, so that the swan wouldn't be upset. They said they knew just how to deal with him.

We went indoors, but we watched from a bedroom window where the swan could not see us. We saw the Speeseeay man and his friend throw some special food to the swan that it seemed to like very much. They kept throwing it, and walking backwards, and the swan followed, eating, right out of Mrs Cocoa's back gate.

They threw more food and more food until they came to the van, and it followed the food up to the van, and up a little plank into the back of the van, and when it was inside, and they had made it comfortable, the Speeseeay man and his friend drove the swan back to the park.

And it was just as well, because next day the snow and ice began to melt away, and the pond turned to water again.

After that, when my sister saw the little green van with RSPCA on it running about the town she always waved to it, and said, 'There goes the Speeseeay man!'

Read more books about

My Naughty
Little Sister

DOROTHY EDWARDS

My
Naughty
Little
Sister

Illustrated by Shirley Hughes

DOROTHY EDWARDS

More
Naughty
Little
Sister
Stories

Illustrated by Shirley Hughes

DOROTHY EDWARDS

My Naughty
Little
Sister and
Bad Harry

Illustrated by Shirley Hughes

DOROTHY EDWARDS

When my
Naughty
Little
Sister
Was Good

Illustrated by Shirley Hughes

DOROTHY EDWARDS

My Naughty
Little
Sister's
Friends

Illustrated by Shirley Hughes

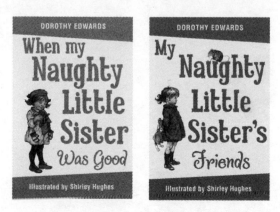